To Barbara, the only You Person for me
D. E.

For Savannah
R. C.

First published 2004 by Walker Books Ltd
87 Vauxhall Walk, London SE11 5HJ

2 4 6 8 10 9 7 5 3 1

Text © 2004 David Elliott
Illustrations © 2004 Randy Cecil

This book has been typeset in Alpha

Printed in China

British Library Cataloguing in Publication Data:
a catalogue record for this book is available from the British Library

ISBN 0-7445-8055-2

www.walkerbooks.co.uk

WALKER BOOKS
AND SUBSIDIARIES
LONDON · BOSTON · SYDNEY · AUCKLAND

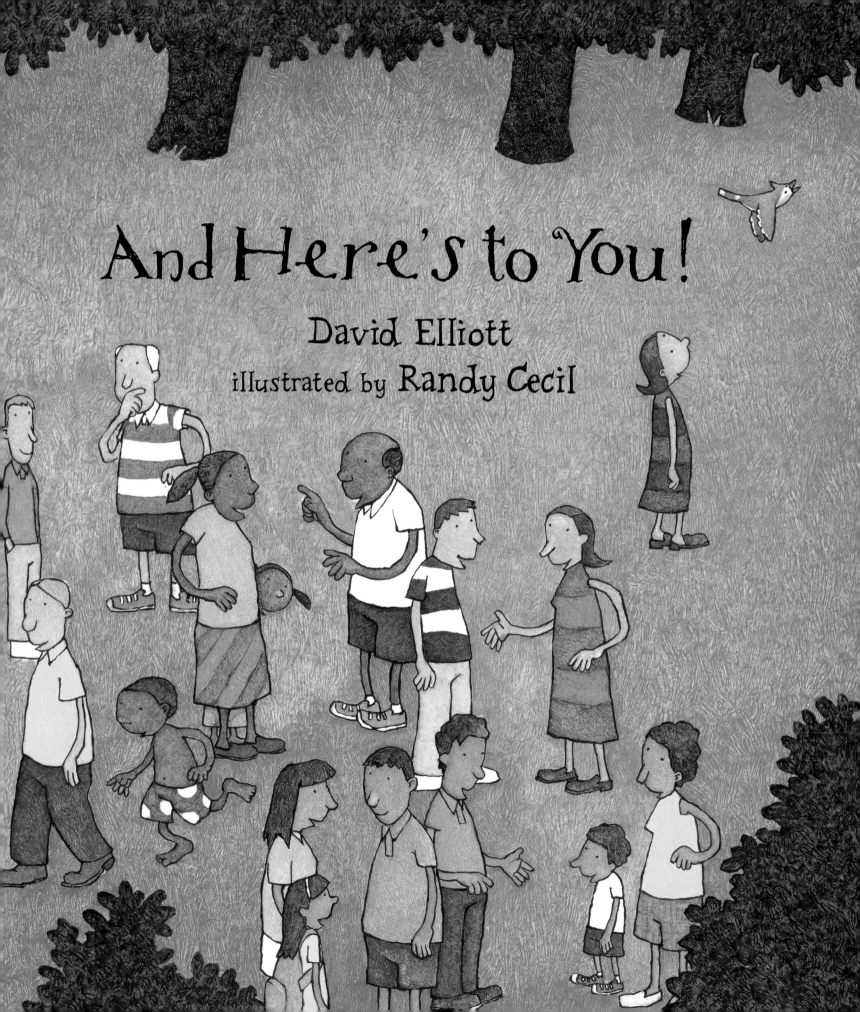

And Here's to You!

David Elliott

illustrated by Randy Cecil

Here's to the birds!

The Feather People!

Birds!

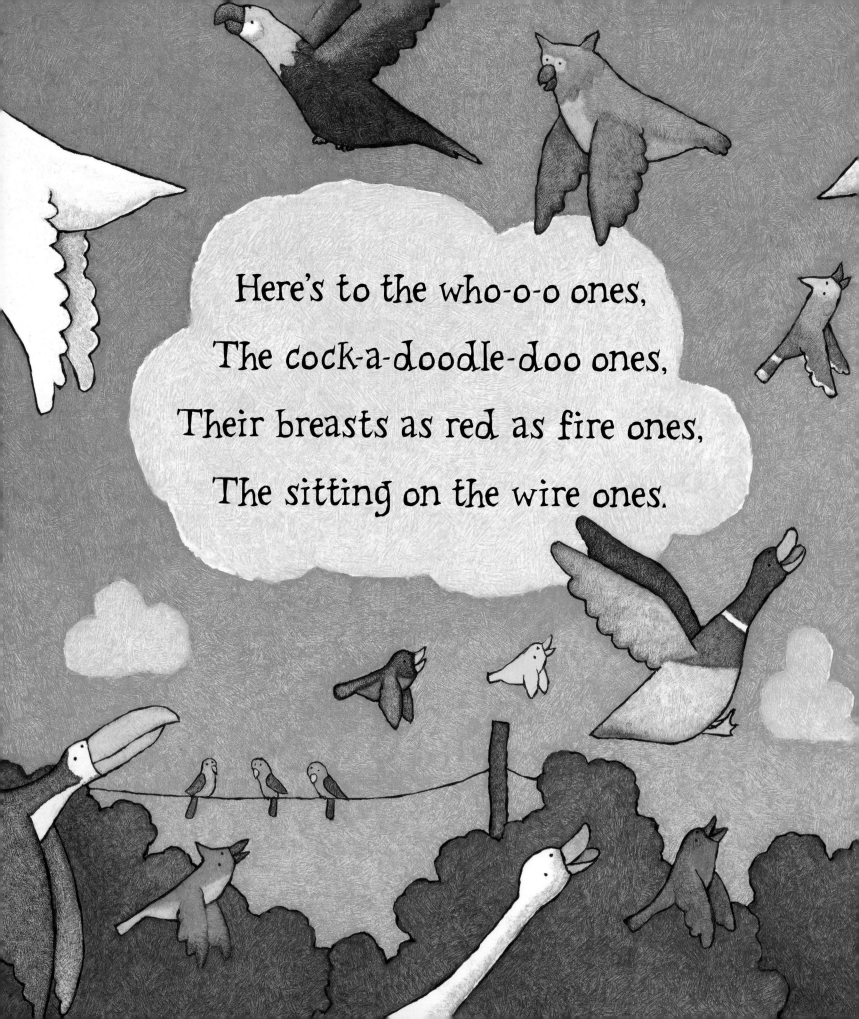

Here's to the who-o-o ones,
The cock-a-doodle-doo ones,
Their breasts as red as fire ones,
The sitting on the wire ones.

Here's to the fish!
The Bubble People!
Fish!
Here's to the spiny ones,
The river and the briny ones,
All slippery and scaly ones,
And finny and fishtaily ones.

Oh, I love the fish!

Here's to the bears! The Hungry People!

Bears!

Here's to the black ones,

The humps on their backs ones.

Here's to the white ones,

The swimming through the night ones.

Here's to the bugs!

The Leggy People!

Bugs!

Here's to the sting-y ones,

The weird and the wing-y ones.

Here's to the fuzzy ones,

The buzzing making honey ones.

Oh, I love the bugs!

Here's to the cats! The Purring People!

Cats!

Here's to the creeping ones,

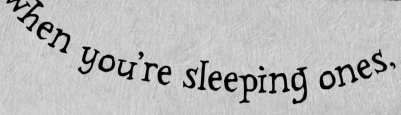

The get you when you're sleeping ones,

The country-wild and city ones,

The KITTY KITTY KITTY ones.

Here's to the dogs!

The Dreaming People!

Dogs!

Here's to the howling ones,

The running, yipping, yowling ones,

The go and fetch a stick ones,

The LICK LICK LICK LICK LICK ones.

Oh, I love the dogs!

Here's to the cows! The Giving People!

Cows!

Here's to the woolly ones,

The bonny and the bully ones.

Here's to the silky ones,

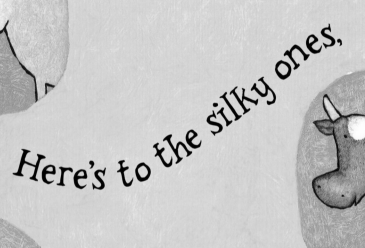

The butter-cream and milky ones.

Oh, I love the cows!

Here's to the frogs!
The Singing People!
Frogs!

Here's to the bass ones,
The big nothing-but-face ones.
Here's to little peeping ones,
And lily pad and leaping ones.

Here's to the people!

The People People!

People!

Here's to the merry ones,

The bald and the hairy ones.

Here's to the mum and dad ones,
And polka-dot and plaid ones.

Oh, I love the people!

And here's to you!

The You Person!

You!

Here's to the sweet you,

The messy and the neat you,

The funny-way-you-eat you,

The head to your feet you,

The total and complete you.

Oh, how I love you!

The You Person!

You!

Yes!

You!

I love you!